Dot.

...

Randi Zuckerberg

ILLUSTRATED BY **Joe Berger**

HARPER
An Imprint of HarperCollinsPublishers

To my son, Asher—thank you for teaching me that life isn't always about rushing forward and looking back but about taking time to stop and simply appreciate the journey

—R.Z.

For Charlotte, Matilda, Bea, and Martha, xxx

—J.B.

This is Dot.

Dot knows a lot.

She knows how to tap . . .

to touch . . .

to tweet . . .

and to tag.

She knows how to surf . . .

to swipe . . .

to share . . .

and to search.

And Dot LOVES to talk . . . .

and talk

and talk

and talk!

But now . . .

Dot's

all

talked

out.

Mom says, "Go outside, Dot!
Time to
REBOOT!
RECHARGE!
RESTART!"

Outside . . .

Dot remembers . . .

to tap . . .

to touch . . .

to tweet . . .

and to tag.

Dot forgot . . .

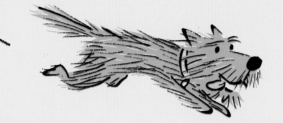

she knows how
to surf . . .

to swipe . . .

to search . . .

and
to share.

Dot still loves to talk . . .

and talk
and talk
and talk!

This is Dot.

Dot's learned a lot.